AF269518

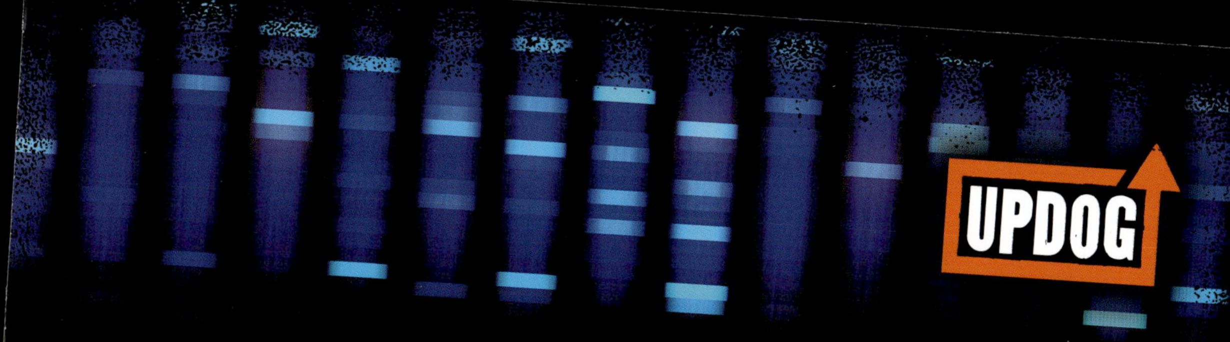

True Crime Clues

CSI CONTROVERSIES

GRACE CAMPBELL

Lerner Publications ◆ Minneapolis

Lerner Publications Company
An imprint of Lerner Publishing Group, Inc.
241 First Avenue North
Minneapolis, MN 55401 USA

For reading levels and more information, look up this title at www.lernerbooks.com.

Main body text set in ITC Franklin Gothic Std.
Typeface provided by International Typeface Corp.

Editor: Rebecca Higgins **Designer:** Kim Morales **Photo Editor:** Rebecca Higgins

Library of Congress Cataloging-in-Publication Data

Names: Campbell, Grace, 1993– author.
Title: CSI controversies / Grace Campbell.
Description: Minneapolis : Lerner Publications, [2021] | Series: True crime clues
    (UpDog books) | Includes bibliographical references and index. | Audience: Ages
    8–13. | Summary: "The case is closed...or is it? Lie detector tests, hair matching,
    and blood splatter analysis pin the crime on the wrong person. Discover the
    controversies of crime-solving and how to close the case for good"— Provided
    by publisher.
Identifiers: LCCN 2019039931 (print) | LCCN 2019039932 (ebook) |
    ISBN 9781541590588 (library binding) | ISBN 9781728401386 (ebook)
Subjects: LCSH: Forensic sciences—Juvenile literature. | Crime scene searches—
    Juvenile literature.
Classification: LCC HV8073.8 .C359 2021 (print) | LCC HV8073.8 (ebook) |
    DDC 363.25—dc23

LC record available at https://lccn.loc.gov/2019039931
LC ebook record available at https://lccn.loc.gov/2019039932

Manufactured in the United States of America
1-47623-48107-12/6/2019

CONTENTS

EVIDENCE IDENTIFICATION
Date
Time
Test For
Case No
DNA/SEROLOGY
DRUGS
FINGERPRINTS
FIREARMS
IMPRESSIONS
QUESTIONED DOCUMENTS
TOXICOLOGY
TRACE EVIDENCE
OTHER
Description of Evidence
Location Collected
Arrest
Seized
Found
Other
Victim/Incident
Remarks/Details
Agency
Signed

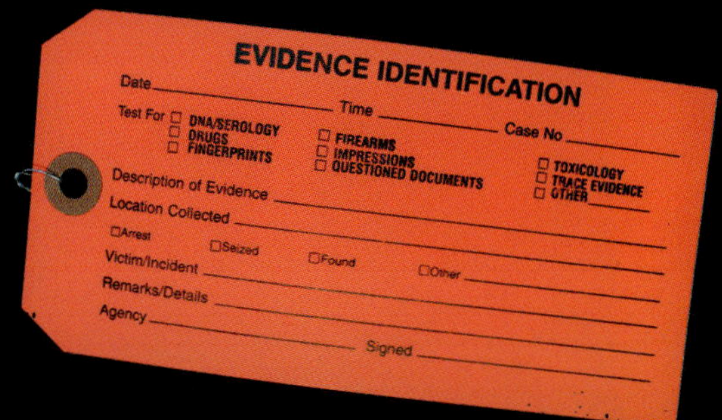

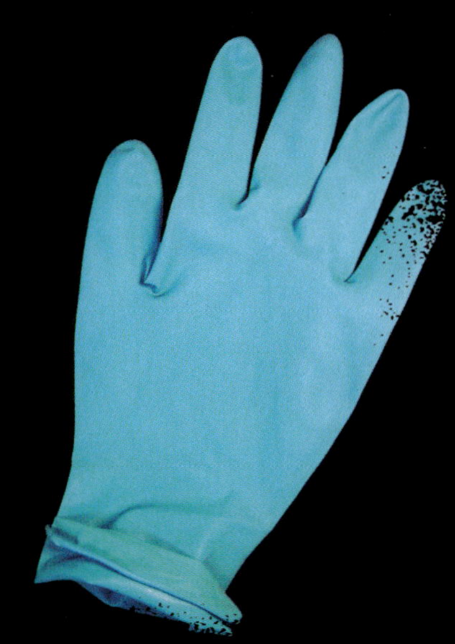

HOW CAN SCIENCE
BE WRONG?

Investigators solve crimes with different techniques. But forensic science is not always correct.

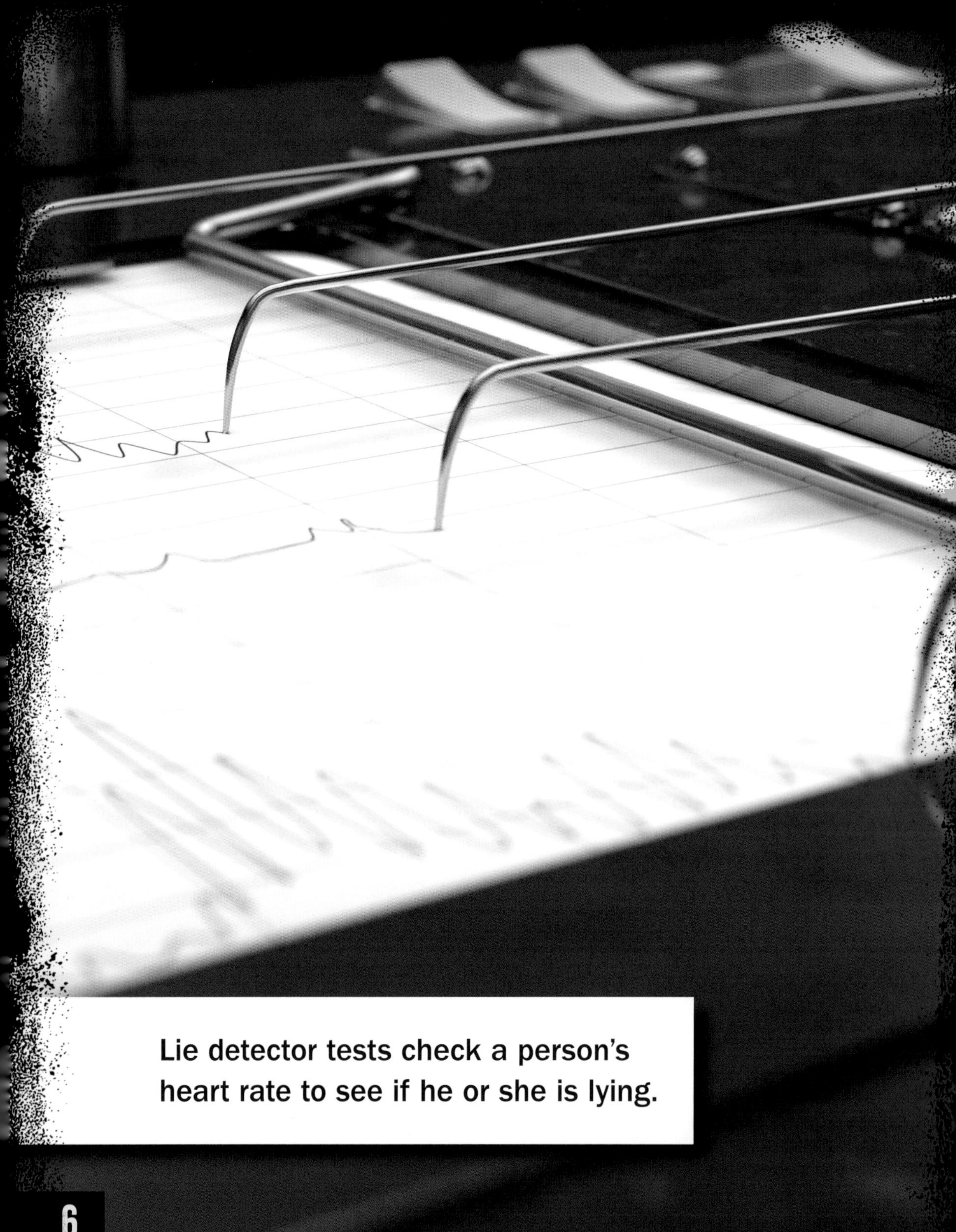

Lie detector tests check a person's heart rate to see if he or she is lying.

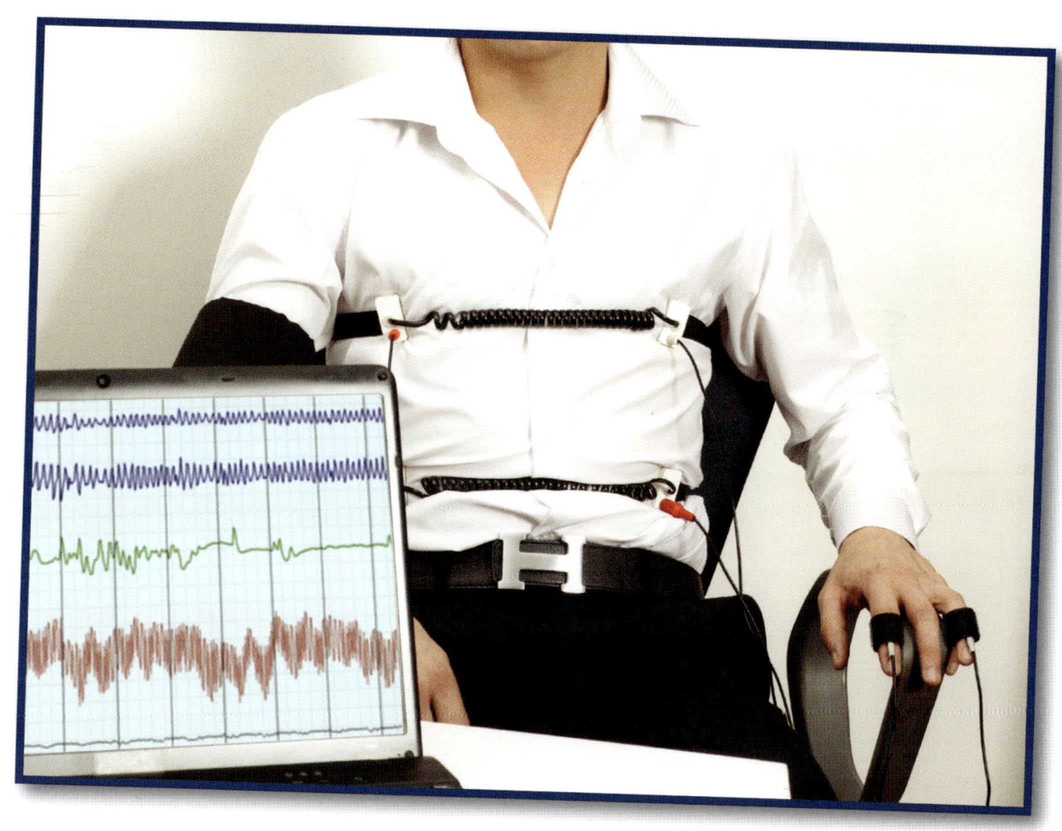

Some people "trick" the test by staying calm.

Blood spatter analysis is not always accurate.

Investigators look at the size and shape of the spatter. They guess what happened.

Fire investigation, hair analysis, and bite marks are unreliable too. DNA is the best evidence to connect a person to a crime.

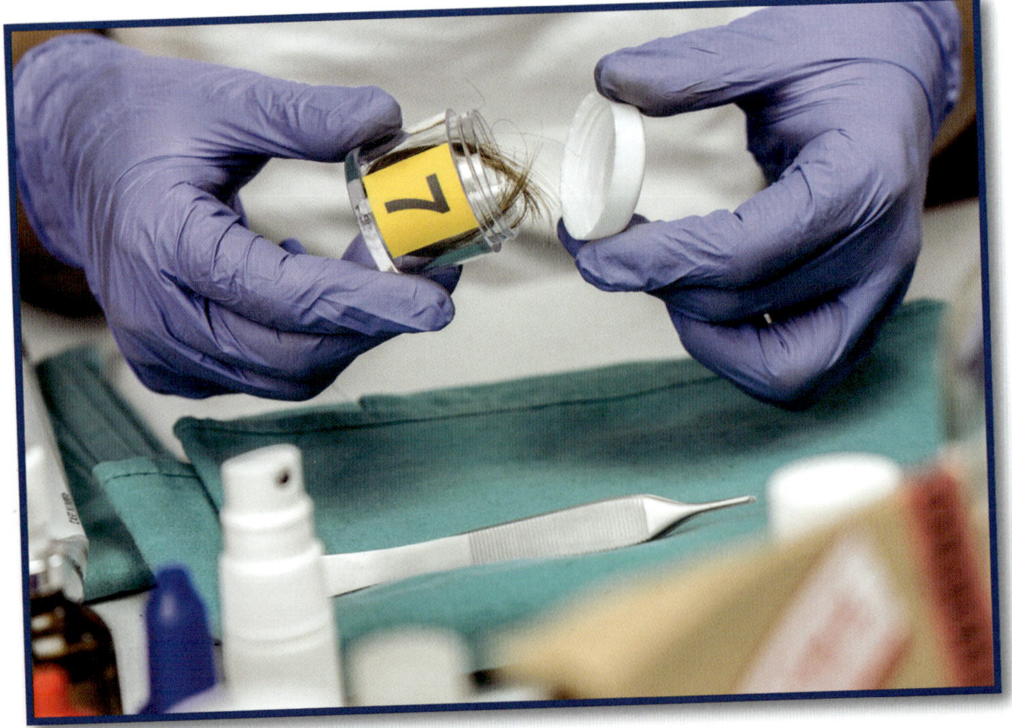

DNA: a substance in cells that carries information

evidence: an object that shows something is true

UP NEXT!

A CASE GONE WRONG.

CASE BREAK!

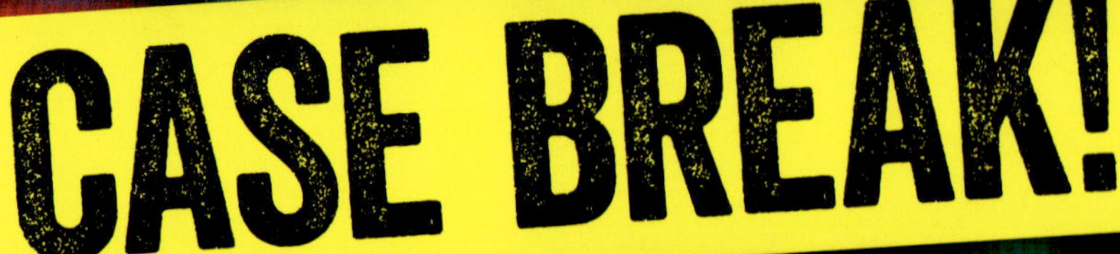

In 1980, Santae Tribble was sentenced to prison for murder. Detectives found hair at the scene. In 2012, scientists found that the hair didn't belong to him.

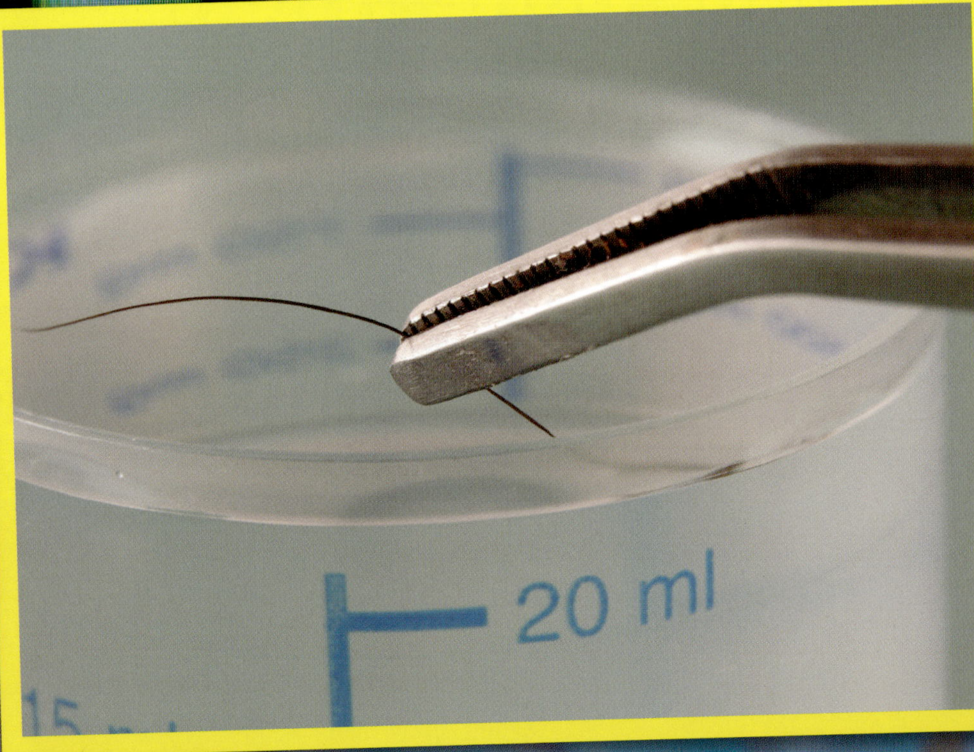

UP NEXT!

THE TRUTH ABOUT FORENSIC SCIENCE.

WHAT'S CONTROVERSIAL ABOUT SCIENCE?

Forensic science standards are still being set.

standards: rules deciding best practices

Some techniques are used before they are
properly tested.

UP NEXT!

MISTAKES AFFECT REAL PEOPLE.

WHAT ARE THE CONSEQUENCES?

Some techniques can have bad results. People can go to jail for crimes they didn't do. Groups work to release these people.

As technology improves, forensic science should become more trustworthy.

YOU'RE THE DETECTIVE

While investigating a crime, you've collected DNA evidence, bite marks, and facial hair from the scene.
Detective, which evidence is most likely to hold up in court?

A. DNA evidence
B. bite marks
C. facial hair

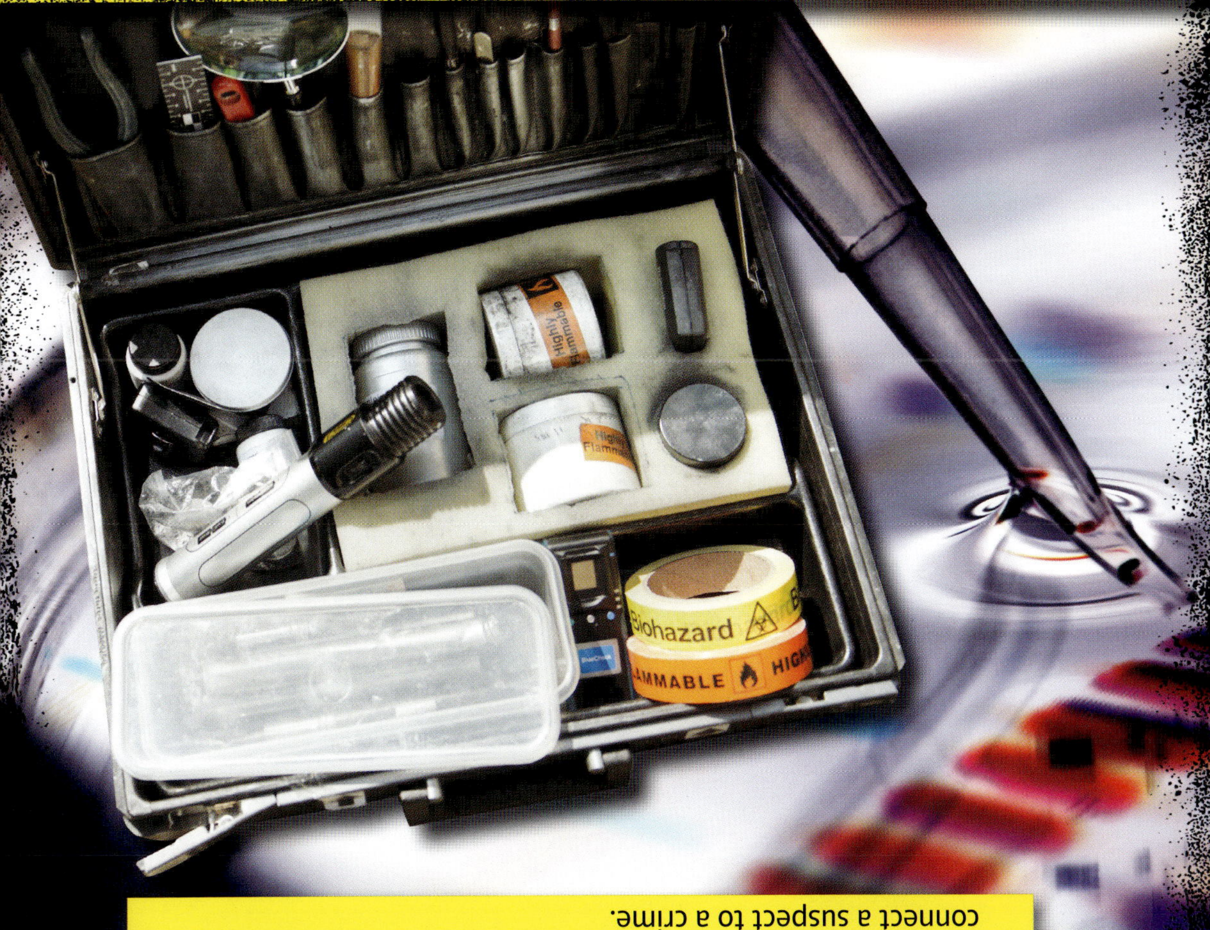

Answer: A. DNA evidence. DNA evidence is the best way to connect a suspect to a crime.

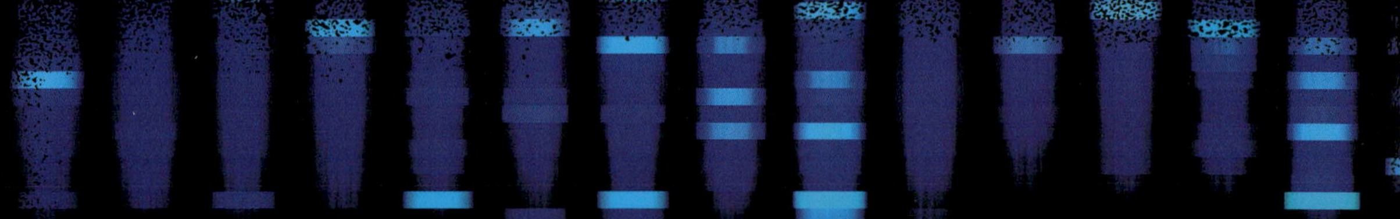

GLOSSARY

accurate: without mistakes

analysis: a detailed look at something to understand it

DNA: a substance in cells that carries information

evidence: an object that shows something is true

forensic: using science to solve legal problems

standards: rules deciding best practices

techniques: specific ways of completing a task

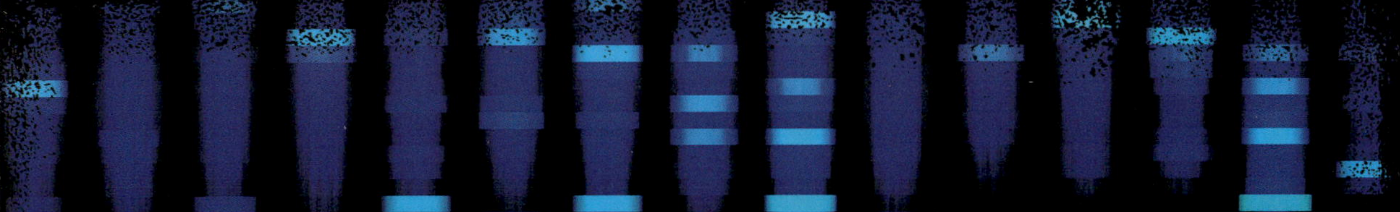

CHECK IT OUT!

Bodden, Valerie. *Lab Analysis*. Mankato, MN: Creative Education Creative Paperbacks, 2018.
Learn about the techniques and technology scientists use to build their cases.

Carmichael, L. E. *Discover Forensic Science.* Minneapolis: Lerner Publications, 2017.
Discover the science behind solving crimes.

Cooper, Chris. *Forensic Science.* New York: DK, 2020.
Explore even more forensic techniques.

Education: Human Lie Detector
https://www.education.com/science-fair/article/human-lie
-detector/
Test your friends' abilities to trick a lie detector test.

Innocence Project
https://www.innocenceproject.org/about/
Find out more about the people overturning wrongful convictions.

Kiddle: Police Facts
https://kids.kiddle.co/Police
Read about the police and their role in solving crimes.

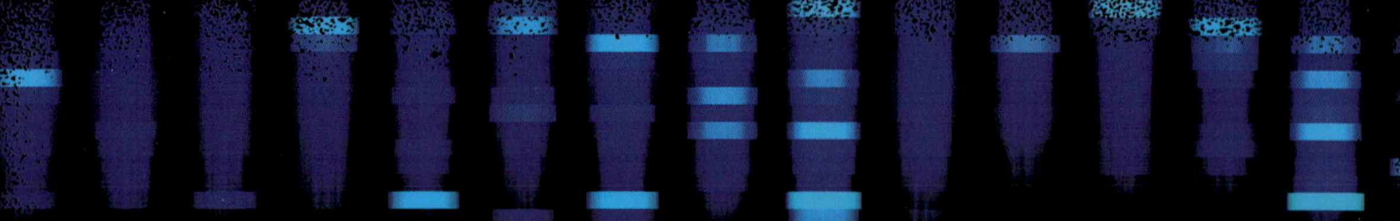

INDEX

PHOTO ACKNOWLEDGMENTS

Image credits: South_agency/Getty Images, p. 4; Milan Markovic/Getty Images, p. 5; allanswart/Getty Images, p. 6; Andrey Burmakin/Shutterstock.com, p. 7; Artfully79/Getty Images, p. 8; stevanovicigor/Getty Images, p. 9; digicomphoto/Getty Images, p. 10; Andrew Brookes/Getty Images, pp. 12 (background), 21 (background); LdF/Getty Images, p. 12; Science Photo Library-TEK IMAGE/Getty Images, p. 14; shironosov/Getty Images, p. 15; Monty Rakusen/Getty Images, p. 16; Chris Ryan/Getty Images, p. 18; BirdofPrey/Getty Images, p. 19; skynesher/Getty Images, p. 20. Design elements: ktsimage/Getty Images; ulimi/Getty Images; jamesjames2541; ABDESIGN/Getty Images; stevanovicigor/Getty Images.

Cover: Standret/Shutterstock.com.